AUTHOR RICH MICHELSON

KILLUSTRATOR SCOTT M. FISCHER

ANIMALS ANONYMOUS

SIMON & SCHUSTER
BOOKS FOR YOUNG READERS
NEW YORK • LONDON • TORONTO • SYDNEY

ANIMALS ANONYMOUS ATTENDANCE

Teacher **Mr. Lewis**
Room **13**
Period/Time **All the time**
Month **Oct**
Year **2007**

Students	Age Appropriate	Anti-Authoritarian	Angry/Argumentative	Attitude Adjustment	Page
1. Camouflaged CHAMELEON	Yes	No	No	?	08
2. ALLIGATOR procrastinator	Yes	No	No	No	10
3. Smart ASS	No	Yes	No	Yes	12
4. The Awkward AUK	Yes	Yes!	Yes	Yes	14
5. BEAR Thugs	No	Yes	Yes	Yes	16
6. BEE Biology	No	No	No	Hmmm...	18
7. Boris, the Boring BOAR	Yes	No	No	No	20
8. Billy, the BULLY	Yes	Yes	Yes	Yes	22
9. Catastrophe CAT	Yes	Yes	Yes	Yes	24
10. The Very Ugly CATERPILLAR	Yes	No	No	No	26
11. COCKamamie	Yes	Yes	No	Yes	28
12. The COWard	Yes	No	No	No	30
13. DOG(gerel)	Yes	No	No	No	32
14. The Eloquent ELEPHANTS	Yes	Yes	Yes	No	34
15. Something's FISHy	Yes	Yes	No	Yes	36
16. Laughless GIRAFFE	Yes	Yes	Yes	No	38
17. Bad News GNUS	Yes/No	Yes	Yes	No	38
18. Hip HIPPO	Yes	Yes/No	Yes/No	Yes/No	40
19. HOG(wash)	Yes	No	Yes	No	42
20. Hoarse HORSE	No	No	No	No	44
21. LAMB on the Lam	No	Yes	Yes	Yes	46
22. Lonely LEOPARD	Yes	No	No	Yes	50

#						
23.	TV LOONACY	YES	NO	NO	YES	52
24.	Unthinking MINK	NO	NO	NO	YES	54
25.	Mighty MITE	YES	NO	YES	NO	56
26.	Holy MOLEY	YES	NO	NO	Hmmm...	58
27.	Itching OSTRICH	NO	NO	NO	NO	60
28.	Shallow OWL	YES	NO	NO	NO	62
29.	RABBIT Habbit	YES	NO	NO	NO	64
30.	The RATional RAT	YES	YES	NO	NO	66
31.	Robin, the Robbing ROBIN	NO!	YES	YES	YES	68
32.	Pimp SHRIMP	NO!	YES	YES	YES	70
33.	The SKUNK That Stunk	NO!	NO	NO	YES	72
34.	The SNAIL Ideal	NO	YES	NO	NO	74
35.	Sneaky SNAKE	NO	NO	YES	YES	76
36.	The Toady TOAD	NO	YES	NO	NO	78
37.	Talking TURKEY	YES	NO	YES	NO	80
38.	WHALE's Spiel	NO	YES	NO	NO	82
39.	The Yakkity YAK	YES	NO	YES	NO	84
40.	The Zen ZEBRA	YES	YES	NO	NO	86
41.	Camouflaged CHAMELEON II	YES	NO	NO	NO	88
42.						
43.						
44.	OBSERVERS					
45.	Word-Maven RAVEN					
46.						
47.	A Dreamer LEMUR					
48.						
49.						

CHAMELEON

Girls treat me like I don't exist.
A virgin? Hell. I'm still unkissed.

Guys say, "I sure would hate to be ya.
Half the time, can't even see ya."

My name's synonymous with wuss!
That's why I took the school bus
to Animals Anonymous.

WHAT'S SAID IN HERE
WILL STAY IN HERE
the sign says.
AT A.A. WE CARE

CAMOUFLAGED

I feel, I say, like a wallflower.
My color changes hour to hour.

It's like I live inside a cloud.
I never stand out in a crowd.

I'm boring, easy to ignore-

THAT'S WHEN THE SHRINK BEGAN TO SNORE!!

But I'll be noticed! They've not heard
the last of me. You take my word!

I'll hide beneath the psycho chair
and write down everything I hear.

The next jerk that ignores my tail—
I've got the goods on them.

BLACKMAIL!!!

ALLIGATOR
PROCRASTINATOR

HEY GATOR!

LET'S FIND SOME ANACONDAS WE CAN FIGHT.

LATER, I SAY.

NOT TONIGHT.

HELP US REARRANGE THE WAY
THOSE CROCODILES SMILE.
LATER, I SAY.
IN A WHILE.

WE GOTTA SHOW THAT OTTER WHY HE OUGHTA LEARN TO PRAY.
LATER, I SAY.
NOT TODAY.

We'll bet that threatening egrets is a thrill you won't forget.

Later, I say.

Not yet.

It's fun to frighten frogs and beat up beavers and raccoons.

Later, I say.

Soon.

Let's terrorize those turtles.

We'll shell-shock 'em. Show you how?

Later, I say.

Not now.

Let's swim around that swamp rat

till his heart pounds and he's dizzy.

Later, I say.

I'm busy.

Join our Gator Gang

and we'll protect your back forever.

No way, I say.

Never.

SMART ASS

It's ASSinine
I'm reASSigned
(well . . . left behind)
to seventh grade.
(Take my word—
they must have erred.
It should be third.)
Hee Haw Hee Haw
I hate to draw,
sometimes I snore
but math's a bore
and art's a chore
Haw Hee Haw Hee
And history's
a mystery.
Do homework? Never!
I'm much too clever.
I'm one smart ASS.
I almost pASSed
chemistry clASS
(I pASSed some gas.)
Hee Haw Hee Haw
My jokes are poor;
not elegant—
don't mean I ein't
intelligent.
Haw Hee Haw Hee
Sure, I'll agree
my spelling stinx.
But still, I thinx
I shoulda made
it to eighth grade.

13

The
Awkward
AUK

I'M AWKWARD EVEN FOR AN AUK.

MY MOM SAID, "YUCK" WHEN SHE KISSED ME.

I SQUEAL AND I SQUEAK AND I SQUAWK WHEN I TALK.

I WADDLE AND SWAY LIKE A DUCK WHEN I WALK.

THE AIR FORCE REFUSED TO ENLIST ME.

SO I FLEW FROM MILWAUKEE TO BROOKLYN, NEW YAWK.

NO ONE I KNEW EVEN MISSED ME.

I JOINED A PUNK ROCK BAND. MY HAIRDO'S MOHAWK.

I SQUAWK WHEN I TALK AND I DO MY DUCKWALK.

NOW FANS GAWK AND GIRLS CAN'T RESIST ME.

I HANGS WITH GANGS
OF BEAR THUGS.
I PLAY ROUGH.

MY BUDDIES CALL
ME SLUGS
BECAUSE I'M TOUGH.

16

I STOMP AND CHOMP
ON BUGS.
I'M NO CREAM PUFF.

I FLEX MY PECS.
I MUGS.
I STRUTS MY STUFF.

I'LL FILL YOU FULL
OF PLUGS.
DON'T CALL MY BLUFF.

BUT WHEN MAMA GIVES OUT
BEAR HUGS,
I CAN NEVER GET ENOUGH.

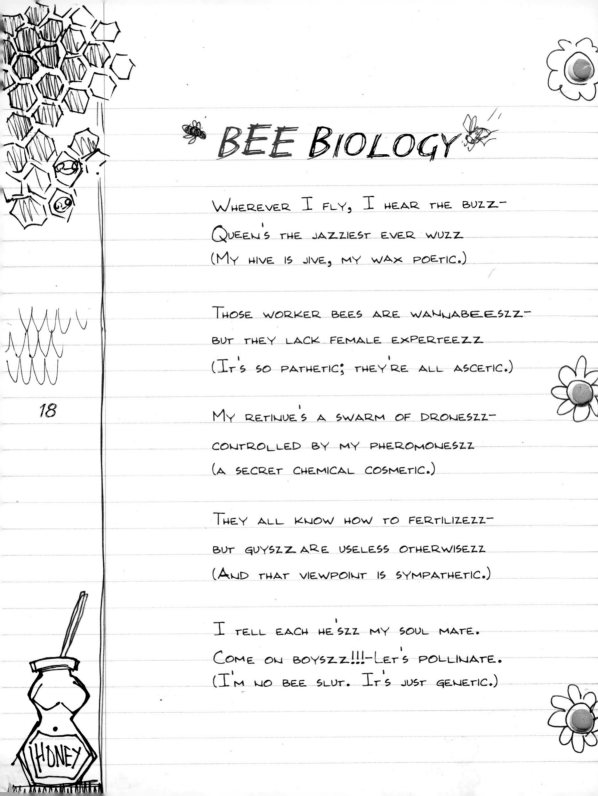

BEE BIOLOGY

Wherever I fly, I hear the buzz—
Queen's the jazziest ever wuzz
(My hive is jive, my wax poetic.)

Those worker bees are wannabeeszz—
but they lack female experteezz
(It's so pathetic; they're all ascetic.)

My retinue's a swarm of droneszz—
controlled by my pheromoneszz
(a secret chemical cosmetic.)

They all know how to fertilizezz—
but guyszz are useless otherwisezz
(And that viewpoint is sympathetic.)

I tell each he'szz my soul mate.
Come on boyszz!!!—Let's pollinate.
(I'm no bee slut. It's just genetic.)

This poem will be boring. I'm Boris the Boar.
I talk and I talk and I talk a bit more.
I talk and I talk about Boris the Boar.
I talk and I talk and I talk till you snore.
This poem was boring. I'm Boris the Boar.

21

BILLY, THE BULLY

I'm Billy the BULLY.
I love busting noses!
My snorts are all followed
by muscle-bound poses.

I'm so full of bull,
I say stepping on toes is
my idea of fun
when I'm not busting noses.

My teachers try kindness.
They say they suppose
my childhood home life
was no bed of roses.

"Bull's-eye!!" I say. Still,
except when I dozes
I'm never as happy
as when I bust noses.

CATASTROPHE CAT

I'm Catastrophe Cat and I'm covered with fleas.
I roll in the mud, and I swing from the trees.
I pee in the pool. I spit in the breeze.
I say what I think, and I do what I please.

Mom says I'm Siamese. Born to be queen.
To dine on fine wine and French poodle cuisine.
"Keep your chin high," she says. "Keep your fur clean."
I'd rather eat dirt and drink from the latrine.

Dad calls me Princess. I couldn't care less.
I wear dungarees. I look dumb in a dress.
I know I lack manners and noblesse finesse.
Guess I've got a different idea of success.

Dad says we're purebreds with long pedigrees.
"Don't mix with mongrels," he says. Mom agrees.
"Or alleycats, strays, or those half-Siamese."
But I plan to play with whomever I please.

THE VERY UGLY CATERPILLAR

I was an ugly little larva. I grew uglier each day.

   Even ugly caterpillars thought me uglier than they.

Daddy said I was a beauty; but what else could Daddy say?

So I turned into a pupa and I hid myself away.

And the days passed, and the weeks passed, and the months passed, and today

I have passed my thirteenth birthday, and I've not been out to play;

and I've never tasted chocolate, seen the sea, or learned ballet.

'Cause concealed inside my chrysalis, I hid myself away.

But before I'm even older, and my cremasters decay,

I'm determined to accept myself, so now . . . without delay . . .

my hairy . . . scary . . . dreary self is coming out. . . . Make way!

Please don't frown or put me down or turn your head away.

Look at me! There cannot be an insect lovelier than I.

But I suspect my time is short. Beauty blooms then dies.

My last words are: *Young larva, don't let your whole life fly by.*

Play today! Don't wait until you are a butterfly.

So much to see! Too late for me!

   I'm doomed, my friends. Good-bye.

COCKAMAMIE

They call me cockamamie.

Or coo coo.

Or crazy.

'Cause I won't cock-a-doodle

when I wake up.

I'm lazy.

I say my clock broke.

Poppycock!

Can you blame me?

I'd rather sleep late

And be called cockamamie.

I'M THE COWard OF COWS.
IT'S UDDERLY TRUE.
EVEN MY SHADOW
IS SCARED OF MY MOOOOOOO.

THE BULLies ALL TEASE ME.
ONE HALLOWEEN NIGHT
THEY DRESSED UP LIKE BUTCHERS.
I COWered WITH FRIGHT.

31

I SHUDDERED.
I SHIVERED.
I QUIVERED.
I QUAKED.

NOW I'M FAMOUS
BEYOND BELIEF.

TURNS OUT I INVENTED
THE MILK SHAKE.

THOSE DUMBBELL BULLS' BUTTS
ARE GROUND BEEF.

DOGGEREL

You ask me why I always drool and slobber,
or why I like to chew on smelly socks?
Why did I bark and growl at the neighbors
then sleep while robbers stole their jewelry box?

Why does water taste best in toilet bowls?
And when I'm at the pond—you wonder why
I wait until I'm standing near some towels
before I shake myself completely dry.

I close my eyes and ponder life's deep questions.
Why, when I see trees, do I need to pee?
Why is my nose wet? These are my obsessions.
The great poets themselves do not agree.

"O why thy dog?" Shakespeare asked in a sonnet,
but never put his paw exactly on it.

32

We elephants are eloquent, industrious, intelligent.
We're kindly, we're sweet, we're light on our feet.

Our size is colossus (from tail to proboscis),
but we're calm and gentle;
we're not temperamental.

Our hearts are enormous. Our hopes and dreams
warm us.

We love entertaining. Don't think I'm complaining.

And yet . . .

WE'LL NEVER,
NO NEVER,
NOT EVER
FORGET
HOW
YOU
WORK
US,
AND
WORK
US,
LIKE
BEASTS
IN
A
CIRCUS.

34

THE
ELOQUENT
ELEPHANTS

35

There's more than one kind of fish in the sea.

There's my big sister,

and then there's me.

I'm sloppy.

She's neat.

I'm rude.

She's polite.

She's friendly.

She's kind.

I love to fight.

She's brilliant at school.

I hate to think.

She never smells fishy.

Most days I stink.

She loves water ballet

like Mom.

I'm like Dad.

I have real bad taste.

I also taste bad.

I nibble on junk food.

Her diet's nutritious.

I'm unhooked

and vicious.

Poor Sis.

She's delicious.

36

65/2269

SAMMY
SMALL
555-SLIME

S.S. FILLET

38

I thought the world funny
when my neck was still short.
I would giggle, guffaw,
Chortle, chuckle, and snort.
I would titter and roar
till I rolled on the floor.
I continued to snigger
even as I grew bigger.
Everything seemed a joke
from the moment I woke.
But when I reached full height
and my neck elongated,
I saw so much I hated
that my laughter abated.
I saw wars fought for oil,
and my brothers recruited.
Plus it makes my blood boil
to see rivers polluted
in pursuit of more money.
And now nothing seems funny.
When you're tall as a tree
you can never not see.
Were I nearer your size,
I could tell myself lies.
I could close both my eyes.

But up high, a giraffe
finds no reason to laugh.

LAUGHLESS GIRAFFE

PEACE

SALE

39

BIRKENSTOCKS

HACKEY SACK
FEVER

BAD NEWS GNUS

I've known some good gnus
and some bad gnus.
But who I like best
I cannot choose.

The good gnus mind their p's and q's
and cut food into bite-size chews.
  The bad gnus brew illegal booze.
  They lose at cards and break taboos.

The good gnus write long book reviews,
And recite love poems to the muse.
  The bad gnus wail and sing the blues.
  At night, they fight. By day, they snooze.

The good gnus use soaps and shampoos.
The bad gnus wax their pool cues.
The good gnus always shine their shoes.
The bad gnus line up for tattoos.

The good gnus pay library dues.
Bad gnus say "screw you" and refuse.

In church the good gnus fill the pews.
The bad gnus cruise the cheap revues.

But sometimes bad gnus grow up nicer
And I've learned that vice versa
The good gnus sometimes turn out worser.

HIP
HIPPO

42

I COOL,
I CHIC,
I SWING,
I SWEET,
I STYLISH.

I TELL YOU NO LIES.

I SMART,
I HIP,
I HUGE,
YOU SMALL.

YOU SAYIN' OTHERWISE?

ONCE I WAS A TEEN FILM QUEEN.

MY TENDERLOINS WERE TAUT AND LEAN.
EACH MORNING I ATE ONE WAX BEAN,
AND EVERY EVENING SALAD GREENS.
AND IN BETWEEN I'D BATHE AND PREEN,
AND PAINT MY TOE HOOVES TANGERINE.
ONCE I WAS A MOVIE QUEEN:
THE LEAN, CLEAN, LONELY MEAN MAXINE.

HOGWASH

BUT THEN ONE DAY

I SPIED MY PORKY MAX, AND NOW
I'M HIS POTBELLIED, SMELLY SOW.
HE'S NOT REFINED, AND WHEN WE DINE
HE GRUNTS AND SNORTS. BUT THIS SWINE'S MINE,
AND WE'RE IN LOVE. I LICK HIS SNOUT;
HE LIKES ME STOUT. WHY NOT PIG OUT?
MAX SNACKS ON HOGWASH. I EAT SWILL.
I STAYED FOR LUNCH. I'M PLAYING STILL.
WE ROLL IN FILTH AND SMUT AND GRIME
AND HAVE A ROLLICKING GOOD TIME.
MY TAIL'S UNCOILED, MY HAM IS SPOILED
I NEVER WASH, MY PEN IS SOILED.

SO IF YOU FEEL LONELY OR MEAN,
PERHAPS YOU ARE TOO THIN, OR CLEAN.

45

HOARSE HORSE

This is oh, so, so upsetting.
Worse than when I was bed-wetting.
'Cause I'd hoped I'd be jet-setting
with the money I'd be getting
when my horse came in.

I've been scheming.
I've been SCREAMING.
But it seems that I've been dreaming.
And there's nothing that's redeeming
when your horse don't win.

I'm in debt. I'm fretting. Sweating.
But there's something I'm forgetting.
Oh yeah, why did I start betting?
It's a vice I'm now regretting
'cause I just can't win.

(I ain't saying it's a sin,
but in the end you never win.)

'59 CADDY BABY!

MY MAMA CALLED ME CUDDLYKINS.
THAT'S WHERE ME PROBLEMS ALL BEGINS.

I SEED HOW TENDER, SWEET LAMBS WORRIED
THEY'D END UP STEWED, KABOBED, OR CURRIED.

LAMB

ON

So's I CHOMPED ON FAT CIGARS
AND HUNG WITH JACKALS. HIJACKED CARS.

THE

WHY TRAIL SOME DUMB ARSE GIRL TO SCHOOL.
I AIN'T NO MAMA'S LAMB. I COOL.

LAM

BUT NOW MY WHITE AND SNOWY FLEECE
IS BEING CHASED BY THE POLICE.

THEY CATCH THE TENDERS AND THE TOUGHS.
So HERE'S MY PLEA TO YOUSE YOUNG ROUGHS.

DON'T BE LIKE ME. MY LIFE'S A MUDDLE.
I SHOULDA GIVED ME MA A CUDDLE.

LONELY LEOPARD

My mother can be very mean.
She scrubbed out all my spots.
She must have stayed up half the night,
Because I had, well . . . lots.

I got up in the morning
To put my coat back on.
I looked into the mirror
And my old self was gone.

I went to breakfast bare-assed.
I sulked, I cried, I cussed.
I screamed: "I'm too embarrassed
To board the school bus!"

I haven't gone to class now,
For nearly a whole year,
I'd rather stay home lonesome,
Than hear my peers all jeer.

I used to think my spots were
too round,
too dark,
too small.
Until the day I woke and found
I had no spots at all.

Sitcoms, talk shows, and cartoons-
I watch mornings, afternoons.

I watch so much Dad says soon he
thinks I'll be completely LOONey.

I tell him that throughout the ages
loons have been called loons, not sages.

I tell him it's LOONacy
to study when there's MTV.

I'm proud to be a LOONatic!
Dad picked up my remote and . . .

CLICK.

52

Unthinking MINK

I'm filthy rich: *Ker-chink! Ker-ching!*
I'm wealthier than queen and king.
I've sold my own home-grown mink coat
For a VCR and a diamond ring,
silk lingerie, and a root beer float,
plus a Rolls-Royce, and a round of drinks.
But I should have thought it through, I think—
'cause here's the problem, and it really stinks:
Minks don't drive cars
or frequent bars.
Minks don't watch movies
or TV.
Minks don't wear clothes
or underwear.
Our food is free.
O, woe is me.
I'm one unhappy billionaire.

MIGHTY MITE

First, God said:
"Let there be light."
Then, in His image,
  He made the Mite.

Eons passed, then centuries,
with no improvement I can see
upon the likes of mighty ME.
Both T. rex and pterodactyl
were far too big to be practickyl.
The dodo and the mastodon
were both too dumb, and now they're gone.
But no experiment was worse
than putting humans on the earth.
They spoil the water; and show no shame.
They foul the air and shift the blame.
They give parasites a bad name.
They preach fine sermons
but live like vermin.
They sow more vice
than fleas and lice.
(Their only plus is they provide
a place mites can suck blood and hide.)

If God ever turns out their light,
Will we be better off?
  We might.

56

Holy MOLEy

Mama fed me earthworms when I was a baby mole.

She chopped them, sliced them, diced them, and sometimes served them whole.

But first she said, "Excuse yourself, give praise, and don't be rude.

We're all of us pursuers, and we're all of us pursued.

Some days we get to eat, and other days we are the food."

I studied hard at school and I met my mole goals.

I furrowed to my burrow and I dug my mole holes.

I grew up happy, healthy, and I got to smell the roses,

But Mama's served up truth each night, right beneath our noses.

No one lives forever. Every body decomposes.

So when the earthworms dine on me, dear God, please rest my soul.

I don't pretend to understand Your ways. I'm just a mole.

Anything you tell me to, I'll do without a question.

But maybe you won't mind a theological suggestion.

Everybody dies. But how 'bout I be the exception?

60

ITCHING
OSTRICH

I'm an ostrich with an itch.
I bitch. I kvetch.

I screech.

I crane my neck to scratch.
I stretch

but cannot reach.

I'm twitching every day.
I still can't reach

that

itch.

Now people come and pay

to watch my dance.

I'm rich.

SHALLOW OWL

I'm Howell the Owl, most brilliant of fowls.
I speak cuckoo and cockatoo.
I never quack, cackle, caw, squeak, cluck, or growl

like really dumb animals do.

I don't meow, bowwow, moo, crow, croak, or howl.
I know how to add two plus two.
I read consonants, and I've studied the vowels:
A-E sometimes Y-I-O-U.

62

I'M HOWELL THE OWL, MOST BRILLIANT OF FOWLS.

I'M CERTAINLY SMARTER THAN YOU.

I KNOW EVERYTHING ABOUT WHAT, WHEN, WHERE, HOW.

I JUST CAN'T RECALL WHOO WHOOO WHOOOO.

FACTS I CAN HANDLE. STILL—I PREFER SCANDAL,

GOSSIP, AND RUMOR. SO . . . WHOOOOOOOO?

63

EXCLUSIVE Christy Cockatoo Goes Coo-Coo CRAZY!!!

INTERNATIONAL Enquirer

ALL NEW! CELEB OOPS

Once I was a cuddly rabbit
with a very nasty habit.
When my mama wasn't watchin', I did things nobody knows.
I looked sweet and soft as cotton,
But inside I felt so rotten,

when my mama wasn't watchin',
I'd be quick and pick my nose.

First I'd roll it soft and gooey,
till it felt sticky and chewy.
When my mama wasn't watchin', I did things that I should not.
Easter morn was fine and dandy.
Jellybean's my favorite candy.

Other days with no one watchin'
I ate lots and lots of . . . snot.

64

RABBIT HABIT

Now I'm older. And much bolder.

Still, I glance over my shoulder.

When my girlfriends aren't watching, I do things they'd never guess.

With my pinkie or forefinger

I explore. Sometimes I linger . . .

And I bet, when no one's watchin',

even you . . . c'mon . . . confess.

65

THE RATIONAL RAT

I'M A RATIONAL RAT

AND I'D RATHER BE FAT

AND WELL FED

THAN HUNGRY AND COLD.

OUT ON THE STREET

THERE'S NOTHING TO EAT.

BUT FILTH, FECES, GARBAGE, AND MOLD.

KITTENS ARE CUDDLED.

THAT'S RATHER IRRATIONAL.

WHY PREFER PURRS

TO MY SQUEAKS?

CALL ME RATFINK

BUT HERE'S WHAT I THINK:

I'LL MIMIC CAT MEOW TECHNIQUES.

O RATIONAL ME!

I'D RATHER EAT BRIE,

JARLSBURG, SWISS,

CAMEMBERT, MUNSTER.

IT MAKES ME SICK

TO DO MY CAT SHTICK,

BUT IT BEATS EATING OUT OF THE DUMPSTER.

67

Robin, the Robbing

ROBIN

I took not a smidgeon.
It must have been pigeon.

(Why wake at five thirty, catch worms, and get dirty.)

Stealing's illegal!
It must have been eagle.

(Hard work's for the early bird. I sleep till three.)

Me? Misbehavin?
It must have been raven.

(Because I sing sweetly, I'm trusted completely.)

Which way did he go?
It must have been crow.

(I take from the wealthy and I give to . . . me.)

I give you my word,
I'm not that kind of bird.

PIMP CUP!

70

GRUNK

PIMP-LIFE

It's all about the bling-bling and the
hos and the fast cars.
Ain't no shrimps chillin pretty as my
neighborhood bros are.
We be bejeweled fools, I wear eighty
pounds hard candy.
Some barracuda mess with me, my
honeys come in handy.
I hand my honeys money, I flash cash
and never skimp.
To survive in this dive, can't be no simpleminded shrimp.

Them wimp shrimps work for plankton.
They be tryin' to do right.
But work's got them too tired to be
partying all night.
They all be chumps. Be pumpin', bumpin'
for minimum wage.
I gonna give them ha ha's,
once I get out of this cage.
See we be free at sixteen, if
plans go without a crimp.
So wait for me. I'll still
be primpin' bait and lookin' pimp.

72

THE SKUNK THAT STUNK

My name is Penelope Uranus Skunk.

My friends call me P. U.

My perfume is one part pee-pee,

And three parts number two

(known also as doo-doo),

seasoned with barfbag stew.

My daddy's name is Bartholomew Olfactory.

We call him B. O.

His aftershave smells like a grave

of the newly departed

whose next of kin just farted.

(Whoops! Now it seems I've started.)

My baby brother is such an embarrassment.

He smells like a rose.

He soaps between his toes.

He washes all his clothes.

I have to hold my nose

when Stinky comes and goes.

73

THE SNAIL IDEAL

When I was just a baby snail, I chose all clothes of blue.
I giggled. "Goo goo ga ga." Mama answered, "Coochie coo."

But as I grew, I knew I looked nice in chartreuse and pink.
And Mama never cared a whit 'bout what the neighbors think.

"Be yourself," she said. "For that's the thing we all do well.
Let no one tell you what to wear when you're in your own shell."

When I was just a baby snail, Dad bought me soldier rattles.
And just before my bedtime I would watch them wage their battles.

But as I grew, he and I brewed pots of rosemary tea,
and perfumed all my dollhouses with passion potpourri.

"Be yourself," my daddy said. "Don't let others presume
to tell you how you should behave when you're in your own room."

When it was time for dating, I went out to meet my fate.
I eyed the hunks and harlots till I spied the perfect mate.

We belched at all the ball games, and we swooned at the ballets.
Together we attended the hermaphrodite soirees.

"Be yourself," my partner said. "Someday you'll be my spouse.
No one can tell us who to love when we're in our own house."

Of all God's creatures, mollusks might not be the most evolved,

Though prejudice, I'm proud to say, is one problem that we've solved.

We never try to impede anybody's natural growth,

Whether they are happy being female, male, or both.

The moral Is: There's No One-way-to-be Morality

The Snail Ideal Is: Be Yourself and Please, Let Others Be

If they named my genus Einstein,

you'd assume I'd be real smart.

And it doesn't take a genius to see why.

If my species was named Feces,

you would think that I was smelly

even with the fastest-selling perfume odor on my belly.

If my order was called Order,

you'd imagine I'd be neat.

If my class were nicknamed Candy, I'd be sweet.

That's why it gives me heartache

to be thought of as malicious

Just because some vicious numbskull

named me Snake.

It seems everyone's forsaken me

because I am called Snake.

Won't you please give me a break?

I've baked you this nice cake.

Here. Let's share.

Come close.

Come closer.

SLURRRP. DELICIOUS!

That was a big mistake.

Did you forget I was a snake?

THE TOADY TOAD

If language were honey,

my words would catch flies.

I flatter with chatter,

I praise to the skies.

I butter them up

with a glimpse of my thighs,

then bat my eyelashes

at other frog guys.

78

I thrill them with trills
from the back of my throat.
If sweet talk was money,
I'd buy a fur coat.

I like my cash cold
and my couture haute.
My face should be placed
on a treasury note.

They know I deceive them.
But no one gets pissed.
When I kiss a toad, well—
that prince, he stays kissed.

My sister's talking turkey.
She says, "Just between us two,
the thing 'bout you that I hate most is
gobbledy gobbledy gobbledy goo."

Mom says, "Let's us be honest
about the way you look.
Your snood, your hair, those clothes you wear, are
gobbledy gobbledy gobbledy gook."

My best friend hurt my feelings
and caused a squibble squabble.
The words I heard her whispering were,
"Gobbledy gobbledy gobble."

I cried, and then got angry,
opened my mouth to shout.
But "gobbledy gobbledy gobbledy"
is all that would come out.

There are lots of good things about being a WHALE.

Nobody pokes me or pulls on my tail.

The ocean's my bathroom. I don't need a toilet.

(My poop comes in colors: red, blue, even violet.)

WHALE'S SPIEL

There are lots of bad things about being a WHALE.

I can't weigh myself without breaking the scale.

At beach surprise parties I'm hard to conceal.

I cause a sea gale every time I exhale.

There are lots of good things about being so HUGE.

I do what I want to. I'm nobody's stooge.

I don't have to exercise or curb my diet.

If I sing too loudly, no neighbor yells, "QUIET!!"

There are lots of bad things about being so LARGE.

I never pay kid's price. It's always full charge.

I get nicknamed Blubber, or Barge Butt, or Sarge.

(Sometimes I forget that my real name is Marge.)

There are lots of good things about being COLOSSAL.

The sharks all avoid me, though my nature's docile.

I spyhop and lobtail, and when I breathe out

I get to blow streams of steam out of my spout.

There are lots of bad things about being GIGANTIC.

It's hard to find boyfriends when I feel romantic.

No one ever picks up my restaurant bill.

(Ten tanks, thanks, of plankton and four tons of krill.)

There are good things and bad things 'bout being a WHALE.

But I'd rather be me than a guppy or snail.

Though they'd rather be them, I surmise. No surprise:

There are good things and bad things about every size.

83

YICKETY-YICKETY YAK!

84

THE YAKKITY YAK

I'm Jack. I'm a yakkity yakkity Yak.
I've oodles of riddles and stacks of wisecracks.
My wit wins me trophies. My puns earn me plaques.
I'm chock-full of bad jokes and clever comebacks.

O.G.
original
grazer

85

I'm Jack. I'm a yakkity yakkity Yak.
I'm no sad-sack slacker. I'm sharp as an ax.
In fact, my act's brilliant. There's nothing it lacks.
My put-downs stop brownnosers dead in their tracks.

I'm Jack. I'm a yakkity yakkity Yak.

The other class clowns are all talentless hacks.
Their taunts are no match for my verbal attacks.
When I'm in the back row, no teachers relax.

I'm Jack. I'm a yakkity yakkity Yak.
My fans throw me apples, and chuck me their snacks.

I'm Jack. I'm a-whack-whack-yakkity Yak.

86

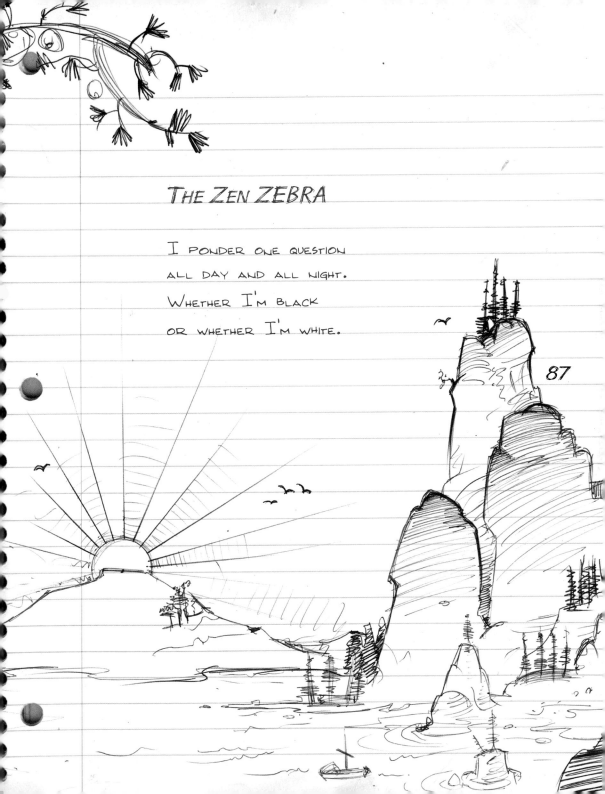

THE ZEN ZEBRA

I PONDER ONE QUESTION
ALL DAY AND ALL NIGHT.
WHETHER I'M BLACK
OR WHETHER I'M WHITE.

87

CAMOUFLAGED CHAMELEON II

I USED TO HATE BEING A LIZARD.
I MADE MYSELF SICK TO MY GIZZARD.

I THOUGHT THERE WAS NO WORSE A FATE
THAN A SATURDAY NIGHT WITH NO DATE.

AT HOME, ALONE, I'D CRY OR CUSS,
AND EVEN AFTER ALL THAT FUSS,
I ALWAYS FELT ANONYMOUS.

BUT AFTER ALL I'VE HEARD, I SEE
MOST BEASTS ARE MORE SCREWED UP THAN ME.

COO-COO!

Instead of feeling alien
I'll praise myself. Chameleons
are wizards. My great skills include:
I can change colors with my mood.

Now I'm less blue. That's pretty cool.
So I think I'll head back to school

and hide this notebook, making sure
my classmates' secrets are secure.

No one but me (and the old shrink)
Will ever know the things we think.

89

About the Author

Word-maven Raven

A baby bird was born in Brooklyn,
Kind, but misbehavin'.
Who knew? He grew—one wife, kids? two—
Into a true word maven.
Smart, no? So-so. Still, now we know
He'd find in books his haven.

He broods a lot and smiles not
Unless he hears you ravin'
About his poems—so take these home—
Your praise is what he's cravin'.

(Plus those book bucks you've been savin'.)

For Marisa the Nerdy Nightingale and Sam the Rambunctious Ram—R. M.

Thanks to Kevin for forcing me to master the Zen of patience while awaiting his calls, but most importantly for saying: "Yes! Awesome! More of that! I love it!" instead of saying, "Are you nuts? Tone it down. I can't publish this."

And thanks to Angela for saying, "I should show this poem to Scott."
And thanks to Scott for bringing this menagerie of misfits to life.

RICHARD MICHELSON is a prize-winning poet and children's book author as well as owner of R. Michelson Galleries, which represents many of children's publishing's most acclaimed illustrators. His numerous books for children have been listed among the years' best by the *New Yorker*, the New York Public Library, The Children's Book Committee, and the Jewish Book Council. *Across the Alley* was a 2006 National Jewish Book Award finalist. He lives in Amherst, Massachusetts. You can visit Richard at www.RMichelson.com.

About the Artist

A Dreamer Lemur

A little lemur, born a dreamer

with a haunting stare,

grew, and as he grew, he drew

and drew and drew and drew and drew

things that weren't always there—

magic, fantasy, sci-fi—

he had a twinkle in each eye

and as he drew he made things new,

he never tried the tried and true,

he broke each visual taboo

and didn't have a single clue.

his friends all thought he'd lost a screw

or two, but now they've changed their view.

Now they know without a doubt

he should be caged, and not let out.

For Teresa Titmouse, Sarah Starfish, and Angela Antelope—S. M. F.

Thank you Madam DiTerlizzi for saying, "Scott, check this poem out."

And thanks to Masters Lewis and Michelson for holding on to this book long enough for me to magically appear with ballpoint at the ready.

And to all the high school "slam books" which have both elated and deflated the ego!

SCOTT M. FISCHER graduated with honors from the Savannah College of Art and Design and is the illustrator of *Twinkle* and Geraldine McCaughrean's *New York Times* bestselling *Peter Pan in Scarlet*. A sampling of the worlds Scott has visited with his illustration work includes Secrets of Dripping Fang, Halo, Harry Potter, Star Wars, Robert Jordan's "Wheel of Time," Magic-the Gathering, and Dungeons and Dragons. Scott lives in Belchertown, Massachusetts. You can visit Scott at www.fischart.com.

SIMON & SCHUSTER BOOKS FOR YOUNG READERS

An imprint of Simon & Schuster Children's Publishing Division

1230 Avenue of the Americas, New York, New York 10020

Text copyright © 2008 by Richard Michelson

Illustrations copyright © 2008 by Scott M. Fischer

Simon & Schuster Books for Young Readers is a

trademark of Simon & Schuster, Inc.

Book design by Scott M. Fischer and Karen Hudson

The text for this book is set in Page Handscript 12/20

The illustrations for this book were rendered in

BIC Pro + pens and Adobe Photoshop.

Manufactured in China

2 4 6 8 10 9 7 5 3 1

Library of Congress Cataloging-in-Publication Data

Michelson, Richard.

Animals anonymous : poems / by Richard Michelson;

pictures by Scott M. Fischer.

p. cm.

ISBN-13: 978-1-4169-1424-2 (hardcover)

ISBN-10: 1-4169-1424-2 (hardcover)

1. Children—Juvenile poetry. 2. Children's poetry, American.

I. Fischer, Scott M., ill. II. Title.

PS3563.I34A55 2008

811'.54—dc22

2007041431

FIRST EDITION